BABAR SAVES THE DAY

First published in the USA 1976 by Random House Inc, New York
First published in Great Britain 1978 by Picture Lions

Picture Lions is an imprint of the Children's Division,
part of the Collins Publishing Group
8 Grafton Street, London W1X 3LA

Copyright © 1976 by Laurent de Brunhoff

Printed by Warners of Bourne and London

BABAR
SAVES THE DAY

COLLINS
PICTURE LIONS

"Today is the day that Olala, the famous folk singer, is arriving in Celesteville," says Babar, the elephant king, to Queen Celeste.

"Just see how excited the children are! They're driving to the airport with their friends."

Pom, Flora and Alexander, along with Cousin Arthur and Zephir the Monkey, stand on the observation deck at the airport. They watch for Olala's airplane. Is it this one? . . . Could it be that one?

The travellers have arrived. Olala is at the top of the stairs with Kawak the parrot, Boho the hippopotomus, and Crax the crocodile.

The children slip through the crowd so they can be in the front row.

Arthur and his friends follow Olala right to the hotel.
But the doorman won't let them in.

"No, no, no!" he says.
"No visitors allowed.
Our guests told me that
they want to rest."

Finally Olala is ready for visitors. Arthur, with the help of Zephir, interviews the famous singer. But Kawak keeps breaking in.

King Babar offers Olala the use
of the theatre in the Amusement
Hall to rehearse
for his concert.

Hidden in the shadows, the children listen quietly while the famous group rehearses.

Suddenly the parrot interrupts Olala's solo with a loud *"Cou-ac! Cou-ac!"*

"No!" shouts Olala. "It's too early. I told you to wait for the chorus."

"I have waited long enough!"

"That's just too bad," says Olala. "*I* am the leader of this group."

"If that's the way you're going to be, I'm getting out!"

Kawak flaps his wings and flies out of the theatre.
Everybody chases after him.

"Kawak, you monster," shouts Olala, "when I catch you,
you will lose a few of those fine feathers!"

Kawak seems to have disappeared, and
now Olala is in despair. "I don't want
to sing without him," he groans. "We
need his *cou-acs*."

"If you can find him," says Babar,
"I will try to talk to him."

Crax asks the gardener,
"Have you seen Kawak?"
"Yes, I saw him," answers
the gardener. "He was flying
that way."

Flora and Zephir ask old Cornelius if he has seen Kawak.
"Yes, I saw him," Cornelius answers. "He was flying
off that way."

Arthur asks the garage mechanic, "Have you seen Kawak?"
"Yes, I saw him," says the mechanic. "He was flying
towards the Grand Square."

Suddenly the Old Lady shouts:
"I see him! I see him!
He is perched on the statue."

Arthur and Zephir scramble
up a fireman's ladder. But
just as Zephir is about
to grab him, Kawak
flies away.

The parrot flies
across the lake.
Arthur and Olala
follow right behind
in a motor boat.

Kawak hides in a cave.
"Now he's out of luck,"
says Arthur.
"We'll catch him."

He's disappeared again!

Where has he gone?

The parrot escapes through a hole at the back of the cave. He flies right into King Babar and Queen Celeste, who are taking a walk.

"How happy I am to see *you*!" exclaims Babar.

The elephant king persuades Kawak to go back with him and talk things over with Olala. "After all," he says, "you like to sing, don't you? And Olala and the others need you very badly."

"Do you really think so?"

"Of course, we need you," says Olala. "I am not angry any longer. Let's forget about our silly fight."

Because so many want to hear the concert, the musicians have to perform outdoors. Olala sings one song after another, and Kawak comes in with loud *cou-acs* during every chorus.

Nobody wants the music to stop. But finally, late in the evening, Olala sings one last song. Everybody claps loudly. The concert has been a big success.

Now Olala and his group have to leave to give other concerts. Babar and his family go with them to the boat.

As the boat glides away
over the Celesteville lake,
Celeste turns toward Babar.

"Tell me," she asks,
"do you *really* like that kind
of music?"

"Of course, I do,"
says Babar. "But I
don't think it needs
so many *cou-acs*."